NOV 29		
JAN 8		
FEB 16		
FEB 24		

THE
CHRISTMAS
GANG

◆ BY JAMES DUFFY ◆

The Revolt of the Teddy Bears
(A MAY GRAY MYSTERY)

The Christmas Gang
(A MAY GRAY MYSTERY)

Missing

Cleaver of the Good Luck Diner

Be Kind to Animals

A MAY GRAY MYSTERY

THE
CHRISTMAS
GANG

• • •

JAMES DUFFY

Illustrated by Barbara McClintock

CHARLES SCRIBNER'S SONS • NEW YORK

Charles Scribner's Sons Books for Young Readers
Macmillan Publishing Company
866 Third Avenue, New York, NY 10022
Collier Macmillan Canada, Inc.

Printed in the United States of America
First Edition   10 9 8 7 6 5 4 3 2 1

Library of Congress Cataloging-in-Publication Data
Duffy, James, date.
The Christmas gang : a May Gray mystery / James Duffy.—1st ed.
p.   cm.
Illustrated by Barbara McClintock.
Summary: While celebrating Christmas together, May Gray's family persuade her to tell them again about her first assignment as a police officer when she solved the mystery of the Christmas Gang.
[1. Poodles—Fiction.   2. Christmas—Fiction.
3. Mystery and detective stories.   4. Paris (France)—Fiction.]
I. McClintock, Barbara, ill.   II. Title.
PZ7.D87814Ch   1989   [Fic]—dc19   88–32762   CIP   AC
ISBN 0–684–19008–7

CONTENTS

ONE ◆ THE FAMILY CHRISTMAS   1

TWO ◆ MADAME SANTA CLAUS   12

THREE ◆ BROTHER AMBROSE   23

FOUR ◆ CHIEF INSPECTOR FLAUBERT   36

FIVE ◆ ROLAND GERSTEIN   47

SIX ◆ THE MASKED BALL   59

THE
CHRISTMAS
GANG

◆ ONE ◆

The Family Christmas

Snow had begun to fall at daybreak. When Baby Bob
awoke, he saw the flakes melting on his windowpane.
Quietly he arose to look out at the park. The ground
was covered with a soft, white frosting. A single set of
footprints led down the street into the park. The city
stretched out silent under the falling snow.

Baby Bob looked into Lolly's room. She was asleep.
"Lolly," Bob whispered. "Lolly, it's snowing." Lolly
grunted and put her head under her pillow.

1

Baby Bob sighed. Maybe Granny May and Victor were awake. He crept into the big bedroom. He climbed up onto the big bed. He peeped under the covers. Victor was snoring, his mouth open. May Gray slowly opened her eyes. "Bob, what are you doing here? Go back to bed. It's too early to get up."

Baby Bob sat on May Gray's stomach. He bounced up and down. "Wake up, Granny May. Look out the window. It's snowing. It's snowing on Christmas!" He scrambled off the bed, kicking Victor in the knee. He ran out of the bedroom. "It's snowing in the living room, too," he shouted. "It's snowing everywhere."

Victor groaned. He sat up and rubbed his knee. He bent over and kissed May Gray. "I told you not to bring those bears into the house, Mama," he joked. "They don't even let us sleep on Christmas. You would think today was something special."

"Well, Victor, why don't you send them off to Tartuffe's Home for Bears? While you're packing their bags, I'll go back to sleep." May Gray snuggled deep under the covers and closed her eyes.

Victor limped into the living room. The snow was coming down hard. Baby Bob was kneeling on the window seat, breathless with the excitement of Christmas and the falling snow. Victor turned on the colored lights of the giant tree, which reached to the top of the ceiling. He wound up the old music box that his parents had played for him on Christmas when he was young. Angels, yellow with age, turned to the tinkling of carols. Victor picked Bob up and held him close on his lap. He kissed the top of his head. *That silly Granny*

May. How could we have a family celebration without Lolly and Bob? It wouldn't be a family without the bears, he thought. He gave Bob another hug.

Bob put his arms around Victor. "Are all your children coming today, Victor? Is everybody coming? Do we open the presents after dinner the way we did last year? I made you something special at playschool." Baby Bob dived under the tree to show Victor a box wrapped in gold paper.

"After dinner, Bob, the same as always. Lolly and I will make the Christmas dinner while you and Granny May straighten up the apartment and look after the family. You'd better go and get dressed. They'll start arriving pretty soon, and we want to have breakfast ready."

As Bob ran off to get dressed, Victor let his memory go back through the years. There had been so many Christmas gatherings, he could no longer keep them all straight. May Gray and he had watched the family grow from year to year, as grandchildren followed children at the celebration. How many were there now? Victor began to count.

There was their oldest daughter, Celeste, and her husband, Philo Montage. Celeste was director of the Royal School of Ballet for Poodles at Versailles. Philo was a famous lawyer. Their only child, Michele (Mikki), was at the university studying politics.

Then there was Richard Gray, two years younger than Celeste, director of a hospital in Lyons. His wife, Maria, was a children's doctor. Their daughter, Simone, was just beginning her studies at the university.

She said she was going to write books for children.

And Mathilde, the baby. Victor smiled to himself as he remembered holding Mathilde in the park every afternoon while they waited for Celeste and Richard to get out of school. Mathilde was much younger. "You will have to look after her most of the time," May Gray had told Victor. "I no longer work on a schedule like an ordinary officer." May Gray was now an assistant inspector. She worked late into the evening. Sometimes she did not come home at all, sleeping on a cot in her office.

How time flies by, Victor thought. Mathilde had grown up too soon. She had married Daniel Duclos; together they owned a small hotel in Nice and almost never found time to come to Paris. Victor had taught her to cook. Now she was the chef for the Hôtel Azur. And she was a mother, too, May Gray reminded Victor, when he fussed about never seeing Mathilde, the mother of three beautiful young children, Ana and the twins Solange and David.

And he mustn't forget the bears, Lolly and Baby Bob, whom May Gray had rescued on her last case, the mystery of the rebelling teddy bears. They had chosen to stay with May Gray and Victor instead of with their friends at the home for bears. Now they seemed more like grandchildren to May Gray and Victor than did the real grandchildren, who only came to visit.

Victor began to add them all up. "Three—and three more. That's six, plus five more. That's eleven. When I count the bears and the grandparents, why, that's fifteen of us." Victor realized that Baby Bob was back and

5

talking to him. "I'm sorry, Bob. I wasn't paying attention. What did you say?"

"Will you and Granny May tell us the story of the Christmas Gang again? That was a neat story."

"I don't know. We'll have to ask Granny May. We told that story last year. Maybe we'll have a vote."

Every Christmas, after dinner and after the presents had been opened, they would all sit around the fireplace while May Gray told them about one of her cases. Sometimes Victor helped. He knew the details of some cases better than May Gray did. Simone was collecting the stories. Someday, she told May Gray, she would make them into a book—or maybe into lots of shorter books for children.

"Come along, Bob. Go wake up Lolly. We have to prepare the breakfast table. We'll let Granny May sleep a little longer on Christmas Day."

Victor went to the kitchen to make the coffee and hot chocolate. He sliced the special Christmas spice bread and the fruitcake. He took the doughnuts he had made the night before from a plastic bag. He put a half a dozen kinds of cheese on the cheese board. Last of all, he filled a large basket with cookies of many colors and flavors, which he had baked the week before. The cookies always disappeared early. This season he had made more than ever.

The doorbell rang. "It's my cousins from Nice," Baby Bob shouted. "I saw them get out of the car."

He opened the door wide and ran back to take Lolly's hand. Mathilde and Daniel and the children piled into the apartment. Daniel carried a giant box filled with presents. He put it down to shake hands with Victor. May Gray came up in her cashmere Christmas gown to hug them all. Baby Bob kissed the twins, which made them cry. Lolly gathered up the hats and coats and scarves and put them on her bed. Christmas had begun.

Within an hour, Richard and then Celeste arrived with their families. They sat around the apartment with their Christmas breakfast plates on their laps, talking about the family. Victor and Lolly put on their green and red aprons to prepare the Christmas dinner. The retired head of Scotland Yard, Sir Waldo Sniffenpooch, had sent May Gray a salmon from Scotland. They had worked together on several important cases. The fish was so large, Victor was not sure he could fit it into the oven. Lolly was preparing a dill-and-truffle stuffing she had learned at cooking school.

The rest of the meal, Lolly and Victor had spent days discussing and, sometimes, arguing about. Lolly had read in an American cookbook a Christmas recipe for squash with maple sugar. Victor insisted that salmon and American squash were not to be considered, but Lolly was determined. Now she was mashing the squash with maple sugar and butter and a touch of fresh nutmeg. Victor took a taste. He smacked his lips. He took another taste. He wiped his whiskers. He bent over to whisper in Lolly's ear, "Don't tell the others, Lolly, but I think I was wrong."

There was also hot vichyssoise soup, fresh asparagus in butter, a chestnut soufflé, country brown bread, and a plain salad. For dessert, Victor had prepared his famous specialty, La Bombe May Gray. For the little children, Bob had made cherry Jell-O with whipped cream.

.   .   .

"I am stuffed," said Philo Montage. "How can you eat so much here, Mikki? You never eat at home."

"Victor and Lolly never cook at home," answered Mikki. "Neither do you or Mother. I am waiting for Lolly to open her café in Versailles so we can stop living on frozen suppers. Mother could send you customers from the ballet school, Lolly."

Celeste smiled. "They wouldn't last long at school if they ate like this, Mikki. I would have to start a school for hippopotamuses."

Ana slipped out of her chair to run into the living room. She began to unwrap the presents. Mathilde went to stop her. "I think it's time to let the children have their Christmas," she announced.

May Gray sat by the tree to hand out the presents. Baby Bob unwrapped a big box. It was a drum from Simone. Bob began to bang as loudly as he could. May Gray and Victor gave Lolly a set of gourmet cookbooks. Richard gave his parents an envelope and slipped out of

the apartment. Inside the envelope was a card and a set of keys. The card said: *The best of Christmas for the best of parents. Look out the window. Celeste, Mathilde, and Richard.*

May Gray and Victor peered through the snow out of the living-room window. Richard was down on the street pointing to a sleek red sports car. He made faces and reached inside to blow the horn. "Merry Christmas!" he shouted up through the snow to Victor and May Gray.

"Oh, boy," said Baby Bob as he scooted for the door.

Lolly grabbed him before he reached the steps. "Come back here, Bob. We'll look at the car tomorrow." She thought a minute. "I think I will go to driving school in the morning and cooking school in the afternoon."

Mikki handed her grandparents another envelope. Inside was a card from the grandchildren and tickets for twelve driving lessons each for Victor and May Gray.

May Gray wiped her eyes. "Thank you all," she exclaimed. "What a lovely gift. I hope Victor can learn in twelve lessons; it will probably take me a hundred and twelve. But I will learn. It took me a long time to become a detective, but I made it."

"That means it's story time," said Mathilde. She gave David to Daniel and put Solange on her lap. "Which story do we get this year? I think I like the case of the red herring. We had salmon for dinner. Let's have red herring for story."

Baby Bob was afraid he wouldn't hear the story of the Christmas Gang. He nudged Lolly, who said, "Baby

Bob wants to hear the Christmas Gang again. Could we take a vote?" she asked shyly.

"No votes," said May Gray. "I know you've all heard it many times before, but let's listen once more, for the bears' sake. Next year you'll have the red herring."

The case of the Christmas Gang had been May Gray's first real case after she'd joined the police. She'd never forgotten the fear and excitement of that Christmas a long time ago when she'd realized for the first time what being a detective really meant.

· TWO ·

Madame Santa Claus

May Gray nibbled on the last cookie, which Ana had
dropped on the floor. She took Victor's hand and
looked at the family gathered around her chair. *Where
to begin?* she asked herself. She had told this story more
times than she could remember, and it seemed she always began in a different way. Compared with some of
her other investigations, it wasn't much of a case at all.
Most of what had happened had been more of an accident than a mystery, but it had made her famous for a

few days and it had made the other officers respect her.

"A long time ago," she began, "Victor and I lived on the Left Bank in one room, which wasn't very big. We had only been married a little while. Victor was studying at L'Escoffier to be a chef. I worked in a bookstore. We were very poor and very happy—almost as happy as we are now." She kissed Solange, who had crawled away from her mother to go to sleep in May Gray's lap.

"Not many customers came into the bookstore, so I had lots of time to read. I liked detective stories best. Sometimes I read two or three a day. I thought I would like to write them myself. I began to keep notes on the back of old white recipe cards Victor brought home from cooking school. But when I tried to put my ideas into stories, they didn't seem to work. Even Victor said they were awful."

"No, no, Mama," interrupted Victor. "I said writers were artists and had to work hard for a long time to be good at what they were doing."

"Well, it's the same thing, Victor. I wasn't very good. I gave up writing mystery stories and went back to reading them. Gradually it came to me that what I really wanted was to become a detective myself. But whoever heard of a female police officer in those days? Victor said maybe I should go to the university as soon as he got a job, but by then I was convinced I had to be a detective. Nothing else would do.

"One day an old police poodle came into the bookstore. He had ribbons and decorations on his coat. There was no one else in the shop and we began to talk. Imagine my surprise when he told me he was Chief

Inspector Flaubert. Everyone in Paris had heard of him. The newspapers reported his every case. Writers made mystery books out of his investigations. There were even songs about Inspector Flaubert.

"When I told him about what I read all day, he began to talk to me seriously. 'Those are just silly stories, mademoiselle. Police work is not very dramatic. It is a matter of experience and routine. Sometimes it is a game of wits, but most of the time you solve a case by persistence—and with some luck.' He was quiet, tapping his nails on a secondhand copy of *Sherlock Holmes* he had been looking at. Then he asked, 'You are very interested, are you not, mademoiselle?'

"'More than anything in the world,' I answered. 'There is nothing I would not give to be a police officer.' I did not dare tell him then I was married.

"I remember that Inspector Flaubert walked to the doorway and looked out at the rain splashing in the puddles. He took off his hat and scratched his head. He pulled at his gray whiskers. He made a face and shrugged. 'Why not?' he finally said. 'Why not?'

"He invited me to come to his office the next day. We talked a long time. He took me to lunch in the police café. He introduced me to his assistants. 'This is Mademoiselle May Gray,' he said. 'If she passes the examinations, she will be joining us.'

"I could see that they did not think much of that. Two or three of them gave me a nasty smile.

"I went home with an armful of police manuals and city maps and ordinances and regulations. Victor left

15

school immediately to be the cook in a brasserie down by the Seine."

"Cooking schools are for learning basic recipes, eh, Lolly?" Victor remarked. "After that you learn everything for yourself. Becoming a chef is like becoming an inspector. Anyway, Granny May and I now had our careers and our lives were set. We didn't see a great deal of each other after that, but we were doing what we wanted to do, and that was important."

"I studied all day and most of the night," May Gray went on. "I wasn't going to let Chief Inspector Flaubert down. I was determined to be the first female police officer in Paris. And I was determined to pass those examinations with the highest scores anyone ever made."

"She did, too," Simone said. "It was in the newspapers. Victor gave me a clipping for my scrapbook. 'FEMALE POODLE SCORES HIGHEST ON POLICE EXAMINATIONS' is what it says."

"I had my badge, but not much else," May Gray continued. "The other officers ignored me or made jokes behind my back. Inspector Flaubert put me on small cases, like finding lost children or missing pets. I didn't care. I just knew I was happy. I knew I was learning, like Victor, what to do. I was familiar with every alley in Paris. I learned where to look for bad guys and how to recognize them. And I was gaining confidence in myself. I told myself I would be chief inspector someday.

"So we come to the case of the Christmas Gang, eh, Simone? Why don't you tell the story now, while I drink my coffee and put Solange on the sofa."

Simone was flustered. Granny May always told this

story. She hesitated. "Just for a little while. It's all in my scrapbook. I'll start and you can go on when you finish your coffee.

"Every year at Christmastime," Simone began, "the detectives took up a collection of money and presents for the Saint-Lazare Orphanage. It was the custom for the newest detective to put on a Santa Claus suit and go to the orphanage to hand out the presents and talk to the orphans. That Christmas it was May Gray's turn. The other officers thought it was very funny. For days before, they called her 'Madame Santa Claus' and made jokes about her. I think it gave them a chance to say things they didn't dare say when she was doing her job.

"Two days before Christmas, it began to snow, just like this morning. That was the day of the orphanage party. Granny May put on the red suit and black boots. She put on the white whiskers and fake eyebrows. She put on her red stocking hat. Then she stuffed a pillow in the front of her pants.

"The other officers were having their Christmas party in the office. They were drinking wine and smoking cigars and being silly. When Granny May came out to get her sack, they all began to tease her. 'Don't forget your reindeer, May Gray,' they said, or 'Don't let the bad guys steal your sled' or 'Don't let the pillow break or you'll be Mother Goose, not Madame Santa Claus.' They thought they were pretty funny. Even Chief Inspector Flaubert made a little joke. 'Watch out for the Christmas Gang, May Gray,' he told her, as he helped her carry the sack of presents down to the police car.

"Although they talked about it every year, the officers didn't really think there was a Christmas Gang. And they never would have known it if it hadn't been for Granny May."

Lolly hadn't heard the story quite this way last year when May Gray had told it herself. "Why not, Simone?" she wanted to know.

"Because all the other detectives couldn't really believe there was a gang that came out at Christmastime and then went away. It didn't make any sense to them, because they had never heard of such a thing before. Granny May says when things don't make sense, you'd better look at them again.

"Anyway, during Christmas lots of rich houses were robbed. For about ten days there was a small crime wave in Paris. It was all very professional. The robbers knew precisely where they were going and what they were doing. They took only cash, expensive jewelry, and small valuables. No one ever came close to catching any of them. The police said it wasn't any gang at all, just more robberies at Christmas because there were lots of parties and people didn't stay home and they were careless during the holidays. Whoever heard of a gang that stopped robbing the day after Christmas?"

"That's enough flattery, Simone," May Gray said. "I'd better go on myself. When you write my memoirs, Simone, I hope you will not try to make me look like Sherlock Holmes.

"There was no reason to suppose that these robbers were organized," May Gray continued. "There is always more crime during holiday seasons for some reason. As I

18

said, what happened was an accident that I was able to take advantage of.

"You see, the police car put me out on the sidewalk about a block from the orphanage. I was supposed to walk down the street and bang on the door of the orphanage, not show up in a police car. The children were watching out the window for Santa Claus. I would say that I left my reindeer down the street.

"The pavement was covered with slippery snow, and it was getting dark. I can tell you that bag was heavy. I was beginning to think that some of the officers had put bricks in the boxes as another joke on Madame Santa Claus. I had to stop and catch my breath. I put my bag down, pulled up my pillow, and arranged my beard.

"At that moment, another Santa Claus came along behind me, carrying a bag almost as large as mine. 'Where have you been, Guillaume?' a voice said. 'Come along. We're late.' The Santa Claus took me by the arm and dragged me down the street before I could catch my breath. Around the corner we went and through a gate into a courtyard. Two other Santa Clauses were just ahead of us. Into a doorway and up some steps, we hurried. I was so surprised by now that I let myself be pulled along without a word.

"The four of us ran into a large meeting hall where wooden chairs were lined up in front of a stage. There were maybe thirty Santa Clauses already seated. At the back of the room was a pile of Santa Claus sacks. We marched up to another Santa Claus sitting with a list at a small table on the stage. By now I was totally con-

19

fused. I did what the others did. 'Bernard, Chief,' said my escort. That Santa Claus at the table checked his list. Nodding to me, Bernard said, 'Guillaume is here, too.' Another check. The other two gave their names. We went to the rear of the hall to deposit our sacks. Then we sat down and waited.

"After three more Santa Clauses had checked in, the chief Santa Claus stood up. 'We are all here now. Let us see what Santa Claus has brought us.' At that moment one more Santa Claus burst into the room. He went up to the stage. 'I'm sorry I'm late,' he reported. 'There was a fire on the Métro.'

"'Your name?' he was asked.

"'Guillaume,' was the reply.

"The chief Santa Claus looked at his list. He turned to the crowd and gazed intently at each face. Then he said, 'We seem to have two Guillaumes here this evening. Will the first one please come to the stage.'

"Bernard shoved me to my feet. I stumbled to the stage.

"'Your name, please,' the chief asked, politely but firmly.

"'I can explain,' I stammered. 'You see, I was on my way to the Saint-Lazare Orphanage and . . .'"

"'Your name, please.'

"'I can't see why you'd want my name,' I replied. By now I was frightened. Whoever they were, these Santa Clauses were serious. I didn't think they would welcome a police officer. I tried a litte joke. 'Just call me Santa Claus,' I said.

"The chief reached out and pulled off my hat and

21

beard. He caught his breath in surprise. Then he gave a tough laugh. 'Are you sure you aren't Madame Santa Claus?'

"'I know who that is,' came a voice from the crowd. 'I saw her picture in the papers last summer. She's from the police. That's not Madame Santa Claus. That's Officer May Gray!'"

• THREE •

Brother Ambrose

"The chief Santa Claus looked at me; then he looked at Bernard, who had come up to the stage. He shook his head. 'I can't believe this,' he said to Bernard. 'After all these years, you brought a police officer here. And a female officer at that. Why didn't you invite Inspector Flaubert and the mayor of Paris while you were about it? Did you reserve us some rooms at the jail for our Christmas holidays?'

"Bernard tried to explain. 'It was dark outside, Chief.

She looked like Guillaume in those whiskers. She was having trouble with her bag, so I pulled her along with me.' He turned to me. 'Why didn't you say something?' he asked.

"I told him that he never gave me a chance. Then I shut up. I thought I might get out if I looked stupid and said as little as possible. The Santa Clauses were upset about something.

"The chief took Bernard and two others to a corner of the stage. They whispered for a long while, looking over at me from time to time. The others sat silent in their chairs, like well-trained children. I sat down on the edge of my chair to wait. I can still remember how hot I was in that pillow and the heavy red suit.

"At last the discussion ended. Bernard and the others returned to their seats. Their chief had calmed down. 'Where were you going in that suit, Inspector Gray?' he asked.

"I told him about the orphanage and how every year a police officer played Santa Claus and delivered a bag of presents to the children there. That seemed to please him. 'Well,' he said, 'we can't let the children at Saint-Lazare down, can we, Bernard? Why don't you be a police officer for a couple of hours? You know a lot about police work, don't you, Bernard?' he laughed. 'Take May Gray's bag and get going.'

"Bernard started to protest but thought better of it. The Santa Clauses didn't seem to argue much with their leader. Bernard shouldered the bag and trudged out the door. 'I am sorry I could not let you go yourself, May Gray,' the chief told me. 'You might come back here with some of your friends before we finished our job. And then someone might be hurt.' He smiled to reassure me. 'You will be quite safe here with us for a couple of days, although you may not be too comfortable.'

"'Well, I have a pillow at least,' I said, and pulled the pillow out of my pants. The chief and all the others broke out laughing.

"'We will get along fine, May Gray,' the chief told me. 'We are all interested in Christmas, each in our own way. We are all interested in orphanages this time of year. You are probably wondering what we are doing here in our Santa Claus suits.' He turned to the others. 'Shall we tell the inspector about our own work?' His companions looked confused, but they nodded yes.

"'I think I will, then,' the chief said, 'since this is the last Christmas we will be together, thanks to Brother Bernard's mistake. It's time someone knew more about us, so long as it's not enough to hurt us. Why don't you get the wine and sandwiches, Brother André? It must be time for our supper.'

"A fat Santa Claus went to the back of the hall. He returned with a canvas bag. He took out large sandwiches of meat and cheese and bottles of wine. I took a cheese sandwich. I devoured it before the others had finished. The chief handed me another. I took a swallow from his bottle of wine. I wasn't as afraid as I had been. My new friends seemed like anyone else, although they didn't talk much.

"'This is a kind of brotherhood,' the chief began. 'We call ourselves brothers. You have already met Brother Bernard and you know Brother Guillaume. You will meet some of the others later on. I am Brother Ambrose. We use our Christmas names. Our real names are of no interest to you. I believe the police sometimes refer to us as the Christmas Gang.'

"Brother Ambrose must have seen me jump with fright. 'There is no need to be scared, May Gray. We are not altogether harmless, but we certainly are not dangerous criminals. Have you ever heard of Robin Hood?'

"I nodded. I wondered if Brother Ambrose was going to tell me that he and his gang of thieves were some sort of modern-day Robin Hoods.

"'Well, like the merry men of Sherwood Forest, we rob the rich to help the poor. For ten days every Christmas, we come together in Paris to play Santa Claus. We take only from the very rich. Each of us has a special charity we look after—an orphanage, a hospital for the poor, an old-age home. We have discovered that no one pays much attention to robbers this time of year, especially if they are not too greedy. Our little system has worked very well so far. Not one of our Santa Clauses has been arrested. Until today, you police never knew that there really was a Christmas Gang.'

"I was so surprised by what Ambrose told me I asked a dumb question. 'What are you doing behind all those Santa Claus whiskers and suits? You don't have to play games to help orphans and invalids.'

"'I regret that we cannot satisfy your curiosity, Inspector. Maybe we are lawyers and clerks or doctors or miners or officials. Maybe some of us are detectives.' Brother Ambrose laughed at his own joke. 'The fact is that very few of us know each other. It is safe this way. We wear our beards and uniforms all the time. None of us has any desire to go to jail.'

"'What are you going to do with me?' I stammered. 'The police will be looking for me soon.'

"'We know that, May Gray. We want you to be our guest while we finish this year's work. Now that you have our secret, there will be no Christmas Gang next year. Perhaps it is just as well. Some of us are tired of spending Christmas away from our families, eating sandwiches and itching in these whiskers.

"'What we want you to do is write a letter to Chief Inspector Flaubert or your husband—I see you wear a wedding ring—which will keep them from worrying about you until the end of Christmas Day. You know what to say. Inspector Flaubert would not hire a dumb poodle to be a detective.'

"Brother Ambrose gave me a Christmas card and a pen. He put a chair at his little table. Then he joined the gang at the back of the hall. I watched them unload their bags of wallets, purses, rings, necklaces, bracelets, pins, and silver and gold table services. Everything was sorted. The money was counted and put in a number of equal piles. The jewelry and other valuables were carefully packed in wooden boxes.

"Brother Ambrose saw me watching. 'I will explain this to you later. Right now, please finish your letter. Remember that if the police come looking for you tomorrow or Christmas Day, we may not be so friendly.' The tone of his voice became harsh.

"I stared at the card. What could I say that would tell

27

Victor I was all right? What could I say that would convince Inspector Flaubert that I wasn't taking time off from my job? I chewed at my pen. The idea came to me that if the detectives remembered the kids at Saint-Lazare every year, I could make them believe I was spending Christmas at the orphanage.

"'Dear Victor,' I wrote. 'I am sorry I will not be home for Christmas. The children at the orphanage never had a Santa Claus spend Christmas with them before. They want to prepare a celebration and a very special meal. They have saved their francs, so tomorrow I will take some of them shopping. Christmas Day we will have a banquet! This is very important to them, Victor, and to me, too. You and I will have a lifetime of Christmases together. Please try to explain what I am doing to Chief Inspector Flaubert. I dare not call him. He would think I am silly and order me back. I love you so much, Victor. Merry Christmas from your wife, May Gray.'

"Brother Ambrose read the letter carefully. 'That will work,' he said. 'You are even smarter than I thought, May Gray. Maybe you should join our gang. Brother Maurice, put on your regular clothes and take this card to Inspector Gray's husband. Tell him you are from the orphanage.'"

Victor interrupted. "That's just what he said. He had a hat over his eyes and stayed in the shadows of the doorway, so I couldn't see his face. When I read the letter, I was very proud of my wife. I told myself that the fancy Christmas dinner I had planned could wait for another year.

"The next morning I spoke to Inspector Flaubert. 'There is no need to apologize, Monsieur Gray,' he told me. 'Your wife did the proper thing. Those kids at the orphanage need a Madame Santa Claus more than we do. Your wife has good intuition. She will be a famous detective someday. And a good mother,' he added. He shook hands with me. 'Merry Christmas,' he said as I left.'"

May Gray took up the story. "You can imagine how embarrassed I felt when Victor told me about this later. I had lied to him and to Chief Inspector Flaubert. But I wasn't thinking only about myself when I wrote the letter. Ambrose and his friends looked very tough. They were not going to be captured without a fight if the police raided the hall. Also, I was beginning to think of other ways to catch the Christmas Gang.

"I went to the back of the hall to look at the loot. Brother Ambrose told me that each Santa Claus received an equal share of the money. He pointed to thirty-five piles of francs. Ambrose and Bernard took care of the jewelry and other valuables after Christmas. They melted down the gold and silver. The jewels they took to a dealer of stolen goods in another country. They divided these proceeds among the brothers. It was a good business, and he was halfway sorry it had to come to an end.

"'How much do your charities receive each year?' I asked.

"'That varies from year to year, of course, but it is usually a large amount.'

"Next, I wanted to know how they knew that each brother didn't keep the money for himself.

"'May Gray,' he answered, 'this is a charitable brotherhood. It is unthinkable that any of us would violate a trust.'

"When Bernard and Maurice returned, Brother Ambrose asked who had jobs to pull that night. Four Santa Clauses took their empty sacks and were checked out on the list. Brother Ambrose sent Brother Gabriel to watch at the gate of the courtyard and told Brother Yves to relieve him at midnight. The rest of us stretched out on the floor to sleep. Bernard gave me two blankets, one to sleep on and the other to put over me. Ambrose lay down by the door. 'Do not be impatient, May Gray,' he said. 'I am a very light sleeper.'"

"Weren't you awfully scared, Granny May?" Lolly asked. "I remember how scared I was when Baby Bob and I were thrown out into the trash can."

"I wasn't alone like you, Lolly. The gang didn't have any interest in me. All in all, they were quite polite. The next morning they gave me some sweet rolls and coffee they brought in. Then they took their bags and went off to work. Bernard stayed behind to guard me.

"Brother Ambrose instructed him to tell me nothing. He did just that. He asked me how I became a police officer, how long I had been married, and questions about myself. When I tried to talk about him or Brother Ambrose or the gang, he smiled.

"That evening they all came back and emptied their bags, had their sandwiches and wine, and went to sleep on the floor. I could not sleep. I knew I would have to answer to Chief Inspector Flaubert. It was time to be a detective, not a captive Santa Claus. I began to put

32

things in order, what I knew and what I didn't know. The trouble was, I didn't know much. Still, until I fell asleep, I tried to work out plans on how to capture the gang.

"Brother Ambrose rang a Christmas bell the next morning. 'Wake up,' he shouted. 'It's Christmas. It's time to celebrate! We have a guest to entertain this year. Let us start early.'

"Ambrose and about half the gang went out. The others straightened up the hall, folded the blankets, and put them in the boxes to cover the jewelry and other stuff. They paid no attention whatsoever to me.

"Before noon the thieves came back. Ambrose was carrying a box with fancy wrapping and ribbons. Another Santa Claus had a tree on his back. The rest carried bags and boxes. Brother René went out to stand guard."

"It's a good thing he did, too," Victor told the family. "I was lonely Christmas morning. Granny May isn't much of a cook. I decided the orphans needed a real chef to help them with their Christmas dinner. It was still snowing, I remember. I put on my boots and made my way over to rue Saint-Lazare. I knocked on the door. I told the matron I had come to help May Gray with the celebration. She looked at me as though I were a lunatic. 'What May Gray?' she demanded.

"I explained that May Gray, my wife, had come two days ago to deliver presents to the orphanage and stayed on to celebrate Christmas with the children.

"'I can assure you, monsieur, that we have no May Gray here. A Santa Claus did come the day before yesterday, as always this time of year. It was no May Gray Santa Claus, sir. I could tell by his voice and his size. He gave out the presents and went away. I know nothing about your wife, sir.' She shut the door in my face.

"I ran home through the snow. I took May Gray's card to the department. I showed it to the officer on duty and told him what the matron had said. I told him I wanted my wife back. He called Chief Inspector Flaubert at once. 'May Gray is missing, sir. I think something has happened to her.' I could hear Inspector Flaubert roar that he would be there in fifteen minutes. He wanted every detective on the force to be there in thirty minutes."

"While this was going on, I was having Christmas dinner with the gang," May Gray explained. "It wasn't one of Victor's meals, but it was quite good; they had brought it in from a brasserie. They had decorated the tree and we sat around it, singing carols. Brother Ambrose gave me a big box. 'For your inconvenience, Inspector May Gray.'

"As I was untying the ribbon, Brother René burst into the hall, shouting, 'There are police down the street at the orphanage. Our truck is ready in the courtyard.'

"The gang went into action at once. They worked fast. Each Santa Claus took his pile of money. They carried the boxes down to the truck. The tree and every other trace of the Christmas party were gathered up and carried away. Even my Christmas box disappeared out the door. I never did find out what was in it. In fifteen minutes the hall was clean and tidy.

"The truck drove off with some of the gang. The others scattered. Brother Ambrose was the last to leave. 'Adieu, May Gray. I hope we do not meet again. Please wait until I have reached the street before you join your friends.' We shook hands, and he ran down the steps."

• FOUR •

Chief Inspector Flaubert

"'We are glad to have you with us again, May Gray,' Chief Inspector Flaubert said, as he leaned back in his chair and unwrapped a stick of gum. 'Are you sure you still want to be a police officer?'

"'More than ever,' I answered. 'I am sorry that I was not able to do more to help capture the Christmas Gang.'

"'Your first duty as a police officer in danger was to protect yourself and wait for assistance. You must remember that, Inspector Gray. We do not need heroes. You did just what you should have done. Now you can go ahead and solve the case. It is all yours.'

"'My case, Chief Inspector?' I asked. You can imagine my surprise. I had been an officer for only six months. I had let myself be captured and held by a gang of robbers. I had let them get away. I had discovered nothing of importance about them. I wondered what Inspector Flaubert was doing. I think I must have decided he'd given me the case because he didn't want to waste one of his more experienced detectives on a long case that was going to be difficult."

Victor spoke up. "That wasn't so, Mama. It was an important case. Simone has the clippings in her scrapbook. What do they say, Simone?"

"They say that the brave Officer May Gray was kidnapped by the Christmas Gang and held captive for two days. They say that because of her, the city of Paris would not be bothered by these holiday thieves ever again. They say that they expect May Gray to bring the case to a satisfactory conclusion very soon. I can show you, Granny May."

"*Pfui!* The reporters had a good story in a dull week and they made the most of it. Inspector Flaubert had to say the right things so that one of his detectives wouldn't look like a fool and disgrace his department. Police don't want bad guys to know that we are like everyone else. Police officers make mistakes, too. It was a good thing I had Inspector Flaubert to help me on my first real case."

Baby Bob was bored by all the interruptions. He

37

wanted to hear how Granny May caught the crooks. "Go on with the story, please, Granny May. Lolly and I want to hear the rest of the story, don't we, Lolly?"

"In a minute, Bob. Mathilde will have to put the twins to bed. They are both asleep now. Richard will put some logs on the fire. Is it time for the champagne, Victor?"

"Why don't we wait until you finish, Mama? We are all feeling drowsy. The rest of us should walk in the park for a bit. Get your boots and jacket, Bob. We'll throw snowballs at the statue of Charlemagne."

Baby Bob grabbed his outdoor clothes and raced down the steps onto the street. He slipped on the snowy pavement and went down on his bottom. Victor helped him up and dusted him off. Bob made a giant snowball. He threw it at the yellow street lamp. Victor took his arm. "At the statue, Bob, only at the statue."

The family walked into the empty park. The wind whipped the snow and icy rain through the creaking branches of the trees. The park was covered with a shining white glaze. "I have not seen a storm like this in Paris for years," said Philo. "It makes you feel afraid to be out on a night like this."

"It was like this that year of the Christmas Gang," Victor told him. "I can tell you that I was frightened for your mother. I was cold and alone and helpless. Well, we should go back now to hear the end of Granny May's story. Bob's pants are already wet. Come on, Bob. I'll carry you on my shoulders."

May Gray had made herself fresh coffee. She sipped it

from the blue mug Lolly had given her for Christmas. It had her initials on it in big white letters. She smiled at her family. "Where was I?"

"Inspector Flaubert had just put you in charge of the case," Mikki reminded her. "You said you weren't very confident about taking it."

"Oh, yes, I remember. Inspector Flaubert asked me what I had already figured out. I told him my biggest problem was to figure out how much of what Brother Ambrose had told me was true. Was the gang really stealing to help the poor and helpless and sick? Somehow, that seemed very important to me then.

"But it was not at all important to Inspector Flaubert. 'May Gray, that does not matter to us at all. For a detective, stealing is stealing. It is breaking the law. The law says certain actions are wrong. The police do not make those laws. We are only responsible for making them work. Let the newspapers decide whether the Christmas Gang is a bunch of Robin Hoods. For us they are thieves and probably dangerous. Our only job is to catch them.'

"'But what do you really think, sir? I need to know,' I persisted.

"Inspector Flaubert unwrapped another stick of gum. He took the old gum from his mouth and put it in the wrapper. 'Personally,' he told me, 'I think they were lying to you and probably to themselves. Maybe they do make donations to charities every Christmas. So do the rest of us. I think they give most of what they take to themselves. From what you have told me, they sound very serious about what they are doing. Professional

40

thieves rob for themselves, not for anybody else. Did they seem like experts to you?'

"'Oh, my intuition told me they were thieves who worked all year-round, or maybe thieves who had retired and only worked at Christmas. They didn't talk much. They knew what they were doing. Only Ambrose liked to talk. For some reason he was having a good time.'

"'What else did you notice, May Gray?' Inspector Flaubert asked.

"'Little things. I didn't see that many of them wore boots, in spite of the snow and ice. Why? And I noticed the shoes they wore. They were expensive. And their accents. I'm sure Bernard is from the south, Guillaume from Brittany, and René from the Basque country. I'm absolutely certain Ambrose is a Parisian. He is different from all the rest. Also, I think he is older than the others.'

"The inspector was interested in that remark. 'Why do you say that?' he demanded.

"'I could see under the edges of his cap and whiskers. His hair is turning gray. Even his Santa Claus suit wasn't like the others'. It was quite stylish. The way he talked was different. When he spoke from the door the first night, it was dark in the hall, and I would have sworn it was a voice in a darkened theater.'

"'We are getting somewhere now, May Gray. Keep going.'

"'I've been wondering how they knew which places to rob, who was rich, who was not at home. Things like that. They really knew what they were doing.'

41

"'Those are good questions, Inspector Gray. How are you going to find the answers?'

"I told Inspector Flaubert that I was going to talk to some of the robbery victims and to the detectives who had investigated the robberies year after year. I wanted to isolate the ones committed by the gang. I was certain there was a pattern they always followed.

"'You may be right, May Gray, but be very careful when you are talking to our officers. They have become fond of you and very proud of you in the last few days. You are one of us now. You don't want them to think they have not made the proper investigations or that you are someone who knows it all.'

"'I understand you perfectly, sir. I only want the details, nothing more.'

"'Is there anything else you want to say?' Inspector Flaubert inquired.

"'I don't think so, Chief Inspector. I am putting everything on little white cards. They help me keep my thoughts in order. I use old recipe cards Victor gave me.'

"Inspector Flaubert laughed. 'Do not get mixed up, May Gray. We do not want to arrest half the chefs in Paris.' He paused. He looked at me closely. 'Aren't you forgetting something important Ambrose told you, something that is probably true?'

"I thought and thought. In my mind, I ran through all the cards I had made. 'I don't know, sir. I think I've covered everything.'

"Inspector Flaubert was very kind and patient with his young officers. 'How do you suppose the robbers get

43

together every year? How do they know where to meet if they are from all over France? How do they know when and where to come back for their share of the jewelry money?'

"'Why, Ambrose tells them. He's the only one who seems to know them all,' I blurted out.

"'Precisely! But think for a moment. Does he write them letters? Does he call them on the phone? Does he send them telegrams? Does he do anything as obvious and dangerous as that, May Gray?'

"'No,' I answered slowly. 'He's too smart to do any of those things. Tell me, Inspector, how does he get in touch with them?'

"'I don't know, Inspector Gray. That is for you to find out so you can tell me. Now, it is your case. Let me know how you are getting along. Take your time. When you need help, tell me. All of us have the greatest confidence in you.'

"I stumbled out of his office, feeling like a fool. I trudged down to the brasserie where Victor worked. We had a sandwich and coffee together. I told him my troubles."

"Granny May was not only the first female detective in Paris," Victor said proudly, "she was also the youngest. When you are young, you get discouraged easily. But she never stayed down very long. She went home to her little white cards. By now, she had hundreds of them. She shuffled them and arranged them and moved them around. Sometimes she threw some of them into the wastebasket. She carried them to police headquarters and brought them home every night.

44

"One evening, she came home to tell me she was making some progress. It was the first time she really talked to me about the case."

"I didn't want Victor to think I was altogether stupid," May Gray said, and laughed. "I hadn't made much progress, but a little bit, maybe. I'd found out from the other detectives that the robberies of the rich homes and apartments did have a vague pattern. True, they took place at any time of day or night, but always as soon as the place was empty. Homes were being watched, that was for sure. The robbers used picklocks to get in, always through the front door. They were quite open about things. They took only cash and small, valuable things they could handle easily. They worked extremely fast. Sometimes the owners were gone for only fifteen minutes.

"And I figured out how Ambrose must have gotten in touch with the gang. I'm sure Inspector Flaubert already knew. He put some kind of a message in the personals column of a particular newspaper or magazine the gang read before and after Christmas. When I asked the Chief Inspector if I was right, he said, 'You are becoming a real detective very fast, May Gray.'

"And I solved the mystery of the shoes. The Santa Clauses wore their suits and beards for a reason. They weren't just to hide behind. I didn't know the whole reason, but I was convinced that they didn't wear Santa Claus suits to rob the houses. Anyone would remember seeing something like that outside or inside an apartment building. They used their Santa Claus suits part of the time and their regular clothes for robberies. They could take off the suits and hats and whiskers in a hurry and stuff them in their bags. Boots were another matter. Too hard to get off and on. And you had to carry your shoes. Boots were inefficient.

"I told all this to Inspector Flaubert. 'This is better than working in a bookstore, isn't it, May Gray?' he asked me. 'Now you can put away your white cards for a while. It's time to go to work on the street. You will need a partner to help you talk to homeowners and go through periodicals with you and talk to anyone who may know something. Most of all, you will need a partner to discuss the case with. Is there anyone you especially want?'

"'Roland Gerstein is my friend,' I told him. 'Do you think he would want to work with me?'

"'Roland would give his right arm to help solve this case,' Chief Inspector Flaubert said. 'Good. It is settled. Out on the street tomorrow, the both of you.'"

May Gray stopped her story. Tears began to fall. She put her head down and sniffled. "What's the matter, Granny May?" Simone asked. "Are you tired? Do you have a headache?"

May Gray wiped away the tears. "No, no, Simone, I'm all right. I was just remembering a long while back. Two Christmases after that, Roland drowned in the Seine, saving a child who'd fallen through the ice. He was my first partner on the force—and the nicest."

46

FIVE

Roland Gerstein

"Roland was almost as young as I was. His father and his grandfather had been police officers. Roland was very proud to be following in their footsteps. Do you remember, Mikki, when you used to come to my office with Victor? You told us you were going to be a detective."

"It's not too late," Mikki said. "If I don't like politics when I finish the university, maybe I'll start following in your footsteps, too."

"I hope so, Mikki," May Gray said. "I'd like to think we were starting a family tradition."

Baby Bob shouted, "Listen, everybody. I'm going to be a detective as soon as I leave the circus."

Victor gathered Bob onto his lap. "You're going to be a bear in bed if you keep shouting like that. Go on, Mama."

"Well, Roland and I had to decide where to begin. It seemed best to deal first with some little things, just to get them out of the way. There was always the chance we might discover something new. Roland went off to talk to the owner of the meeting hall, while I agreed to make the rounds of stores and brasseries to find out where the Santa Clauses bought their food and wine.

"By the end of the day, we had discovered nothing of value. The owner of the meeting hall lived in another section of Paris. He had been renting the hall to a certain Maurice Gabin for the last eight years. Monsieur Gabin always made the arrangements by phone. He paid the rent in cash, always delivered promptly in advance by a messenger. He told the owner he and his friends used the hall for a Christmas charity. The owner assured Roland that they were very good tenants and left the hall cleaner than they found it. After that, Roland located three Maurice Gabins. He was positive none of them was Brother Ambrose.

"I had no better luck. The sandwiches and wine were bought at various places on rue Saint-Lazare. A Santa Claus would leave an order by phone in the morning and pick it up in the evening. Nothing out of the ordi-

48

nary. The brasseries were used to filling large orders at Christmastime. I could not find out where their wine came from.

"Roland and I looked at each other. 'That takes care of some loose ends,' said Roland. 'We knew we wouldn't find anything, anyway. What next? Brother Ambrose or the periodical files?'

"'How about the robbery victims next?' I suggested. 'I have the police reports fresh in my head. Could we go together? I've never done this before.'

"'I'm no help, May Gray,' Roland Gerstein replied. 'I've been on the same kind of lost-doll cases you've been on.'

"'At first we found out only what we already knew. The places that had been robbed all belonged to rich owners. They could not remember having seen anyone suspicious near the building or on the street. They had usually left the house or apartment to go to a party or to a store. A few had gone away on vacation. They'd came home to find their money and jewelry and small valuables missing. The police had come, listened, asked questions, looked around, and gone away. That was that.

"The break in the case came quite by accident. We were talking to a Madame Angier on rue de la Pompadour. She had lost a collection of rare gold figurines. Nothing more had been touched. She looked at us and said bitterly, 'Why me? There are twelve other apartments in this building, most of them more elegant than mine, I'm sure. And imagine! That very morning a

49

Santa Claus had given me a rose. He said it would bring me good luck the whole Christmas season. I was robbed that very night.'

"I saw Roland prick up his ears. 'A rose? What kind of a rose, Madame Angier?'

"'Just a white paper rose. You see a lot of them at Christmas. They are cheaper than real ones in winter.' She went into the dining room and came back with a large paper rose in a stem vase. 'Here it is.'

"Roland examined the rose carefully. He handed it to me.

"'Why did the Santa Claus give you this rose?' he asked.

"'Oh, I stopped to give him some money for whatever charity he was begging for. I gave him quite a lot, fifty francs. He thanked me and pinned the rose on my coat. He said it was for good luck.'

"Now I began to see a few things clearly. 'Could you show us your purse and coat, Madame Angier?' I asked.

"She returned with a luxurious mink coat and an elegant silk purse. 'Did you have a lot of money in your purse, madame?' I inquired. 'Could your friendly Santa Claus have seen inside it?'

"'I suppose he could have. I had just taken a lot of money out of the bank to buy presents for my grandchildren. I must have taken the fifty francs from that. But how . . . ?' she began.

"Roland Gerstein pointed to the rose. He stood up. 'Thank you very much, Madame Angier. You have helped us a great deal. We will do our best to recover your figurines. Let's go, Inspector Gray.'

"Roland danced his way down three flights of stairs, with his hat on sideways like a silly schoolboy. 'So, May Gray, that's how they did it. Not with mirrors but with white paper roses. Two Santa Clauses set up shop some-where—probably in a fashionable district—asking money for some fake charity. When Santa Claus Number One saw a fat wallet or purse or a mink coat, he pinned on a rose. His partner was nearby. He fol-lowed the rose, while the first Santa Claus followed far-ther back. They got out of their suits, found out where the victim lived, and waited. They were very patient, I must say. Now what are we going to do, May Gray?'

"I told him we had to prove our theory. For the next two days, we went down our Christmas Gang list, ask-ing about the white rose. Everyone on the list had been given a white rose by a Santa Claus. We went back to records from earlier years. We got the same answer.

"Chief Inspector Flaubert took us to Victor's brasserie for lunch. He told Victor to bring a fancy wine. 'This is a celebration,' he said. He put his arms around our shoulders. 'The rest should be easy. Why don't you start on the newspaper files to see if May Gray is right? Don't worry about where the paper roses come from. You can buy them anywhere. They make them in orphanages,' he growled.

"We began with *La Presse*. No luck. We went through *Le Jour*. No luck. We found lots of strange mes-sages, but none of them seemed to be what we were looking for. The back files of the two other daily papers told us nothing. Roland grimaced across the library table. 'May Gray,' he said, 'maybe we are being stupid.

We are starting at the wrong end. Let's go outside.'

"It was bitter cold that January. The streets were still icy. Roland led me to a newsstand. 'What do you see, May Gray?' he asked.

"I was shivering from the biting cold. My teeth shook. 'I see a lot of magazines and newspapers, Roland. What do you see?'

"'A lot of newspapers and magazines, the same as you. Which ones of these have personals columns and are at every newsstand in France?'

"I pointed to a copy of *La République*, a copy of *La Vie Française*, and a copy of *Notre Jour*. 'There must be others,' I told Roland, 'that I am not familiar with.'

"'Let's start with these. They print all sorts of messages and advertisements in the back pages. They come out every week. They are sold at every newsstand in the country.'

"We went back to the library files. I started with *La Vie Française*, and Roland, *La République*. In half an hour, he said, 'Listen, May Gray. This is in the issue of October thirty-first, last year.' He read, 'Paris meeting hall available for charities, December tenth to twenty-fifth.'

"'That must be it,' I said. 'Go back to the beginning of the year. Let's see how they distributed last year's loot.'

"'I'll start with March. It must take Ambrose and Bernard at least two months to convert everything into cash.' He started going through back issue after back issue. 'Nothing,' he grumbled. 'I've gone all the way up through September. Should we try another magazine?'

"'No,' I said. 'I have a crazy idea. Forgive me, but I am trying to think like Brother Ambrose. When was Easter last year?'

"Roland was a perfect partner. He did not call me a lunatic. 'I don't know. I'll go find out.' He came back in five minutes. 'The reference librarian says it was April fifteenth.'

"'Let's count back forty days, Roland. Where does that put us?'

"Roland took out a pocket calendar from his wallet. He carefully counted. 'March sixth,' he announced.

"'And in the personals columns for early February?'

"Roland argued, 'They couldn't have sold the stuff that soon.'

"'You said two months, Roland. March sixth is more than two months. Ambrose knew what he was doing. He had been doing it for years. He may have had to put the ad in earlier. It's all part of his plan. Please look for a message.'

"Roland went to work. In a few minutes he gave a great shout, 'Listen, May Gray: "Masked charity ball at Hôtel Vendôme, March sixth. M. Gabin." How did you know?'

"'I guessed, Roland. There are only a few times a year when you can wear costumes and masks without being noticed. At Christmas, the gang put on Santa Claus suits to become robbers. And just before Lent, there are masked balls and costume parties all over Paris. What better way for Ambrose and Bernard to pay off the gang?'

"'But the charity ball at the Vendôme is a very fancy

affair, May Gray. It is for high society, not robbers.'

"'We are dealing with at least one very fancy crook, Roland. Ambrose is an actor as well as a robber. I am convinced of it now. When we want him, I don't think he will be hard to find. See if he always uses the Vendôme for these payoffs.'"

Baby Bob was trying to stay awake. He squirmed in Victor's lap. "When do we get to the part about the pirates, Victor?" he murmured.

"Pretty soon, Baby Bob," said May Gray. "Victor, you go on while I put Bob in his pajamas and get him a glass of chocolate milk."

"All right, Mama," said Victor. "I know this story as well as Simone and you do. Well, Roland went through seven years of *La République*. He found the same ad. He took May Gray's police overcoat off the hook. 'It's time to visit the Hotel Vendôme. There's no point in going to the magazine's office,' he said. 'All we'd find would be a messenger and cash.'

"Monsieur Fresnay was director of functions at the hotel. He was very happy to talk about a job he enjoyed so much. He told the two officers that the masked charity ball was the biggest occasion the Vendôme put on each year. Thousands attended. Thousands were turned away. The hotel charged five hundred francs for a ticket, which they gave to hospitals and orphanages in Paris. 'We make our money selling champagne and petits fours,' he explained.

"'Do you think it's the same crowd every year, Monsieur Fresnay?' asked Roland Gerstein.

"'Oh, yes. We have a long waiting list for tickets. They are very hard to obtain. Sometimes they are reserved years in advance. This is a very traditional affair in the social life of Paris.' Monsieur Fresnay was quite pleased with his masked ball.

"Roland went on with his questions. 'Do you sell groups of tickets to large parties? For example, do you have someone to whom you sell thirty-five each year?'

"'Indeed we do. That would be Maurice Gabin. He reserves thirty-five year after year. He always sends a large donation along with the money for the tickets.'

"'He sends a messenger with the money, does he? Have you ever met Monsieur Gabin, sir?' Roland went on.

"'Not exactly,' replied Monsieur Fresnay. 'He always calls to make the reservations. And, of course, I would not know him at the ball. No one is supposed to know anyone else, until the end. That is part of the fun. But I sort of feel that I know him. Each member of his party always wears a white rose.'

"Granny May pounced on this at once," Victor said proudly. 'His guests don't really have tickets, is that right? Your staff admits anyone wearing a white paper rose, right, Monsieur Fresnay?'

"'That is true. How did you know it was paper?'

"'Monsieur Gerstein and I know almost as much about these guests of yours as you do,' Granny May said. She showed him her police badge. 'Would I be correct, Monsieur Fresnay, if I suggested that Monsieur Gabin's guests never stay to the end?'

57

"'That is also true. They disappear by ones and twos during the ball.'

"Next, Granny May wanted to know what kinds of costumes Monsieur Gabin's guests wore. Monsieur Fresnay told her the costumes alternated: One year they were all pirates; the next year, hooded monks.

"Next, she wanted to know how Monsieur Fresnay thought he knew which one was Maurice Gabin.

"'One of them carries a bag each year. He gives away all sorts of favors to his party—little boxes, a jeweled handbag, a clown's cap, a cigarette case. I think he must be Monsieur Gabin.'

"'I think so, too,' Roland said. 'Tell me, Monsieur Fresnay, when is the masked ball this year?'

"'In just eight days, February twenty-seventh, to be exact.'

"'Is it a year for monks or pirates, Monsieur Fresnay?' Granny May wanted to know.

"Monsieur Fresnay thought for a moment. 'This year it's pirates. Yes, I'm sure. It's pirates,' he told them proudly.

"Roland Gerstein smiled at May Gray. 'Good. We'll take two tickets, Monsieur Fresnay.'"

• SIX •

The Masked Ball

Baby Bob was wearing his new Santa Claus pajamas. He gulped down his chocolate milk. He bounced up and down on Victor's lap. "The pirates, the pirates," he repeated. "I want to hear about the pirates, Granny May."

The rest of the family took up the chant. "The pirates, the pirates. We want the pirates. Tell us about the pirates, Granny May." They clapped and laughed until May Gray waved for them to stop. "For shame.

You are behaving like children. You will wake up the twins and everybody else in the building. Be still and listen. I have almost finished."

"When Roland and I reported to Chief Inspector Flaubert, he didn't say much at first. He unwrapped five sticks of gum and put them on his desk side by side. He studied them for a while. Next he piled them on top of each other. Then he put them all in his mouth at once. He leaned back and stared at the ceiling while he chewed. Finally, he turned to us. 'It looks as though I hired the two best detectives in Paris. Just imagine picking up thirty-five crooks at the Hôtel Vendôme during the biggest event of the season. I wouldn't trade jobs right now with the premier of France.

"'All right, May Gray, what are we going to do? Shall we take them all at once or pick them off as they leave the hotel? And what about Maurice Gabin? It's still your case, May Gray.'

"I told him what Roland and I had decided. We would locate Maurice Gabin, but we would not do anything to arouse his suspicions. Roland and I would attend the ball in mask and costume. The police would quietly pick up the gang as they left the hotel. Ambrose would be the last to leave, we were sure. Roland and I would like to arrest him at the ball.

"Inspector Flaubert agreed. 'But if you don't mind,' he said, 'we will have a few more officers in disguise on the floor—just in case things don't work out the way they should.'

"It was late when I went home. I told Victor everything that had happened. I was too excited to go to sleep. I remember we sat on our shabby sofa in our little room and looked at the lights of Paris until I fell asleep on Victor's shoulder.

"Roland Gerstein wanted to know how we were going to locate Maurice Gabin without letting him know we were on to him. 'If he is an actor, do you think he is a stage actor or a movie actor or both?' he asked. 'Is he acting at the moment, or melting down silver and gold, selling off the jewelry, and getting ready for the big payoff? He's kept himself out of sight for eight years, May Gray. Maybe it's not going to be as easy as you think.'

"'Maybe not, Roland,' I replied. 'But consider how much we already know about him, or think we know about him. He lives in Paris. He is rich, or close to being rich. He is middle-aged, at least. He likes to run things himself. He remains anonymous. Obviously he can't work as an actor from December first until after the charity ball is over. In effect, he is more of a master thief than an actor. No producer would be able to put up with his schedule or demands. Besides, I don't think he wants to show his face to too many people. He doesn't want the gang to know who he is. Bernard is the one who takes care of that part of the business.'

"'So you think he runs a small theater company, is that it, May Gray?' Roland asked.

"'Yes. He probably owns the building as well. He hires his own company, acts when he chooses, and runs his gang, which pays for the theater. Shall we go to the library and see what we can find in the theatrical files?'

"We went through the library files, looking for anything we could find about plays, actors, openings, and closings. We read interviews, studied photographs, collected all the gossip. Roland wrote in his little black notebook. I wrote on my little white cards. From time to time, Roland shook his head. From time to time, I got up from my chair and walked over to the window, to clear my thoughts as I stared down at the melting ice and snow. It was turning warmer outside now.

"'This Maurice Gabin keeps himself well hidden, May Gray. I can't find much that really fits together.'

"'That's because you are not working with cards, Roland,' I teased him. 'Give me the name of someone suspicious, and I will show you how they work.'

"'All right, May Gray. Let's make a bet. If you find him with your cards, I'll rent you your costume for the ball. If I find him with my notebook, you will have to rent mine. Agreed?'

"'Agreed, Roland. Give me a name.'

"'Well, there is an Alain Roget, who might be the one. He owns a theater and only works from time to time.'

"'No,' I answered. 'I know who you mean. Nothing else fits.'

"'How about Marcel Martin, then?'

"I nodded. I arranged my cards. Marcel Martin owned a small theater—the Théâtre du Lys—on the Left Bank. About seven years ago, he had begun to fix it up and to put on more elaborate plays. He produced and directed the plays himself. From time to time, he appeared as an actor. He allowed himself to be photographed only in costume and makeup. He seemed to be middle-aged. He gave very few interviews. He let student groups or amateur companies use the Théâtre du Lys in the winter months. There was no indication of where he lived.

"'Well?' Roland wanted my answer.

"'I win, Roland. It's Marcel Martin, I am certain of it. Listen to this.' I told him what my cards said. 'I will give you some white cards for Christmas next year. Why don't we go down to the Théâtre du Lys?'

"We walked down to the theater. The billboards announced a university-student play, which had just ended its run. The theater looked unused, but there were lights at the windows of the upper stories. We crossed the street for a better look.

"'It's an apartment, May Gray. Three guesses on who lives there. Shall we wait to see what he looks like?' Roland asked.

"'I don't think so, Roland. Let's be surprised on February twenty-seventh. Let's go pick out our costumes. There's a theatrical shop down the street. Are you still paying for mine?'

"'I guess so, even though I did give you the right name to check out on those silly white cards. What are you going to be?'

"'We had better see first what is left. All the good costumes are probably rented by now.'

"The manager showed us a hundred different costumes. None of them seemed just right for the final act of our first real case. Then Roland spied a pirate suit at the back of the shop. It had black pantaloons, buckled shoes, a shirt of many colors, a wide red sash, a bandanna and eye patch, and a long, fake sword. I nodded yes.

"'We'd like two pirate costumes,' Roland said.

"'I doubt that I have two left,' the manager answered. 'I rented thirty-five this week to my best customer. Let me see what is in the storeroom.' He came back with two costumes in a box. 'These are the last two, sir. You will not need alterations. All of our costumes may be adjusted, even the shoes,' he told us proudly.

"Two days before the masked charity ball, Chief Inspector Flaubert made careful plans with his officers. He had a number of disguised police cars and vans ready to put in position around the Hôtel Vendôme. He ordered strange costumes for the officers who would be in the ballroom. Everyone laughed when he told us he had rented a walrus suit for himself; it was the only costume he could get into.

"The evening of the ball was clear. The snow had gone at last, and there was a distant touch of spring in the evening air. Roland Gerstein and I joined the crowds that pressed into the giant ballroom of the Hôtel Vendôme. Under our sashes, we had each hidden a white paper rose. From the mezzanine, the orchestra was playing dance music. Roland and I danced slowly around the floor. The crowd was growing by the minute. We saw costumes from the wildest dreams—monsters, devils, prehistoric beasts—costumes from books and movies, costumes from almost every country in the world. The ballroom was filled with color, gaiety, and music. I had never been close to such an occasion before. I remember how much I wished I were dancing with Victor until midnight.

"Here and there, Roland and I saw a pirate dressed exactly like ourselves. Each of them wore a white rose tucked in his sash. They glanced at us as we danced by, but when they saw we had no rose they paid us little attention. The pirates were not dancing or drinking champagne. They were drifting through the crowd, looking and waiting.

"By eleven o'clock, the ballroom was filled. At midnight, the masks were to be taken off and costume prizes awarded. When was Brother Ambrose going to arrive? Suddenly Roland nudged me. At the end of the ballroom, standing by the velvet draperies, we saw another pirate. He was not dressed like us or the gang. We drew closer. He wore flaring purple pantaloons, gold-buckled shoes, silver hose, a black-and-silver-striped shirt, a black bandanna, and a purple eye patch. He had an earring in his left ear and a heavy gold chain around his neck. He carried a bag of shimmering silver cloth.

"The other pirates casually went up to him. He smiled and clapped each one on the back. He reached into his bag and took out a favor. Each favor could hold a bundle of francs. They were all different.

"Then the pirates began to disappear from the floor, one or two at a time, slowly and easily. By a quarter to twelve, Brother Ambrose, Roland, and I were the only pirates left in the ballroom. Ambrose folded up his bag and made his way to the champagne tables.

"Roland and I now took out our roses and pinned

them to our sashes. We went up to stand on each side of Ambrose, who was lifting a glass of champagne to his lips. Roland asked, 'Don't you have a favor for us, too, Maurice?'

"Ambrose looked slowly at the two of us. He put down his glass. He smiled sadly. To me, he said, 'Aren't you going to introduce me to your friend, May Gray?'

"We led him to the street. A big walrus was waiting outside the hotel. 'Welcome, Monsieur Gabin,' he grunted. 'Perhaps you will want to join your friends? They are waiting for you at the jail.' He put handcuffs on Brother Ambrose and pushed him into the back of a police car.

"It did not take long to learn the history of the gang. It was really very simple. Ambrose and Bernard had put the gang together. Bernard was a clever thief who came out of jail and found a job as a stagehand at the Théâtre du Lys. He and Ambrose hit it off at once. Ambrose had a criminal imagination and great dreams for his theater, which he couldn't afford. Bernard had dreams for a foolproof scheme for robbing.

"Bernard gathered the gang from all over France. He located his friends from prison, he read police reports, he drifted around the tough sections of cities, he talked to thieves who had retired. He chose very carefully. He convinced them that Ambrose's scheme would work. They met early one Christmas season eight years before. Ambrose put on his Santa Claus suit and explained the operation to them in detail. They spent a few days trying it out. Bernard was right. It worked perfectly. The next Christmas, they went at it in earnest. They made a lot of money. After that, many of them worked only at Christmastime. All of them spent the next ten years in prison. And that is the story of the Christmas Gang."

"Not quite," said Simone. She turned to face the family. "You should see my scrapbook. Victor gave me all his clippings. You should see the stories about Granny May and Roland Gerstein. There were pictures on every page. They made Granny May and Roland put on their pirate suits for a set of pictures in color. They both were famous."

"Enough of this silliness, Simone. Within a week, we were both forgotten. I was lucky, lucky to have a chief inspector who supported me and doubly lucky to have a partner like Roland Gerstein, who helped me become a real detective. Get the champagne, please. We'll drink our toast to the memory of Roland."

"I can't," said Victor. "Baby Bob is asleep on my lap. Philo, you get the champagne."

Philo brought in the champagne. There was a loud pop when the cork flew out of the bottle. Baby Bob woke up. As the family lifted their glasses and sang "Auld Lang Syne," he closed his eyes and snuggled back into Victor's arms.

"That was a good story," he said. "I like Christmas a lot."